FABRIC ART FUN

Acknowledgement

The authors, Carolyn Davis and Charlene Brown, would like to thank all of the following for their patience and support — Sally Marshall Corngold, Jim Paine, Kassie and John Raley, and, of course, Sydney Sprague, editor, and the rest of the wonderful staff at Walter Foster Publishing, Inc.

ISBN 1-56010-059-1

Introduction

Fabric art is a lot of fun! People usually don't think of using fabric when they want to make an art project, but we hope this book will change that because working with a variety of fabrics will allow you to be extra creative.

Traditionally, fabric art is called 'functional art" because when the art is finished it has a function or use. We believe <u>all</u> art is functional because it brings pleasure.

Working with fabric will help you to develop your tactile (touch) and visual skills. You will get experience imagining a project and then seeing it come together just as you had pictured it. And, although some of your art projects might turn out differently than you had anticipated, it will still be fun! The more art projects you create, the better you will become at predicting how a project will turn out. This is a great way to learn while having a good time!

Remember, the most important lesson we can teach you about art is to use your imagination and, of course, **have fun**!

Glossary

ABSTRACT — A style of art work with little or no attempt at pictorial representation. This means that instead of making art that looks like an actual thing, such as a cat or a landscape, an artist tries to paint his or her emotions or state of mind. In this book abstract art is used primarily as decorator or fashion art.

ARRANGE — To place the various parts of your project in a certain order. It is helpful to arrange the parts before you actually glue or attach them together to make sure the project will look the way you want it to.

BLEED — When paints spread out and/or run together, creating various effects, shades, or even other colors. For example, when yellow and blue bleed together they make green.

COLOR SCHEME — A combination of colors that are pleasing or exciting to you. There are no right or wrong color schemes, they are simply a matter of choice.

DESIGN OR LAYOUT — The arrangement of the parts and the decorations of your fabric art project.

DETAILS — A small part of the whole project. The details are what make the project unique.

MEDIA (MEDIUMS) — Various materials used to create art. Acrylic, puff paint, fabric and pencils are all different mediums. Every project in this book is a "multi-media" project because each one uses more than one medium.

TEXTURE — The way a surface looks or feels. In this book you will use a variety of textured fabrics.

THREE-DIMENSIONAL — Having the characteristics of height, width and depth. A square drawn on a piece of paper is flat, or two-dimensional, but a real box, such as a cardboard box is three-dimensional. Most fabric art projects are three-dimensional because the fabric itself has depth (or thickness).

Contents

1 Games and Fun Things 9

2 Gifts 27

3 Holiday Fun 37

4 Art You Can Wear 51

Materials

Note — These are some of the materials that are used throughout this book. You do not need to buy all of them. See the instructions for the particular projects you want to make for the materials you will need.

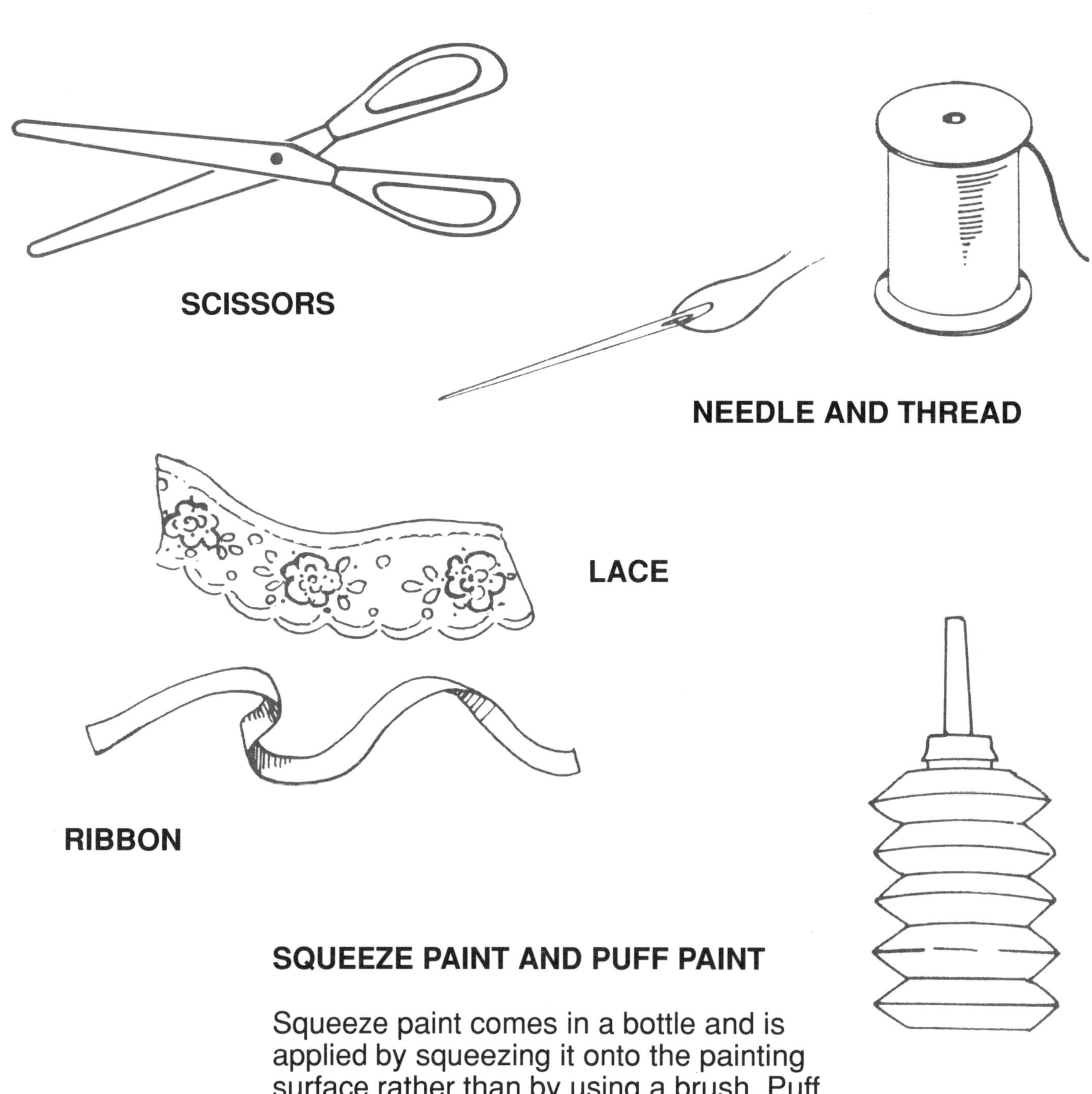

SQUEEZE PAINT AND PUFF PAINT

Squeeze paint comes in a bottle and is applied by squeezing it onto the painting surface rather than by using a brush. Puff paint is like squeeze paint, but it puffs up when it comes in contact with air. These paints can be found at art & hobby stores.

Materials, continued

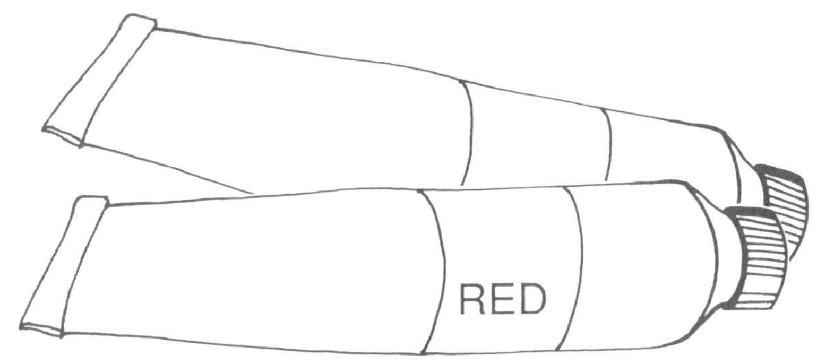

ACRYLIC PAINT

Acrylic paints are water-based and dry very quickly. They are packaged in tubes and come in many colors.

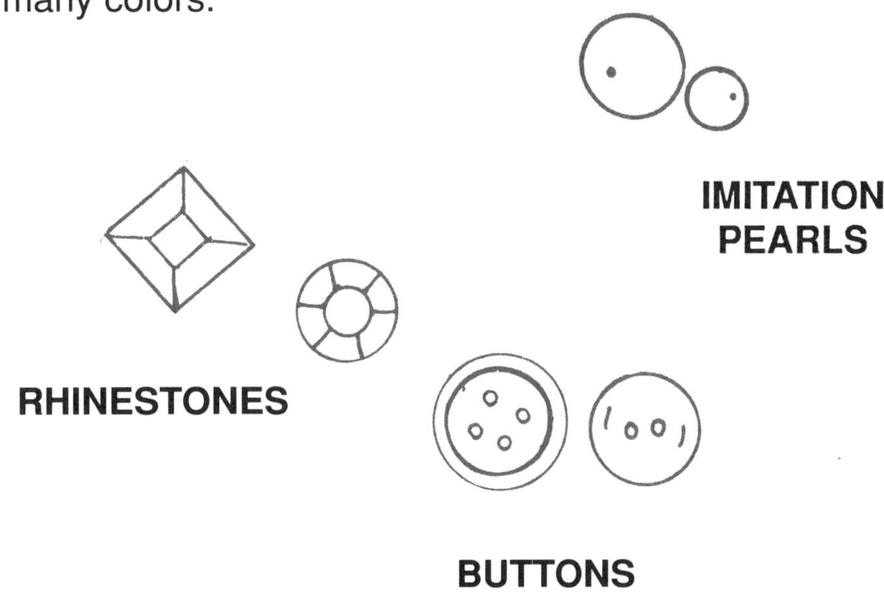

IMITATION PEARLS

RHINESTONES

BUTTONS

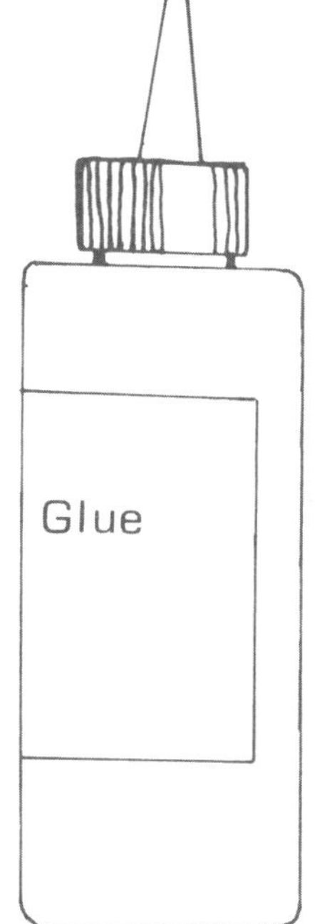

FABRICS

You might need felt, ribbon, lace, yarn, canvas, or nylon fabric (depending on which projects you choose to make). These materials can be purchased at most fabric, craft, or art & hobby stores.

WHITE GLUE

1

GAMES AND FUN THINGS

When people think of art they often assume that making the art is the only fun part. But what if the project is a game? or a puppet? Then you can have the fun of creating over and over again — first, when you make the project, and then every time you play with it. For example, in this chapter we make a dinosaur sock puppet (but, of course, you can make any type of puppet you wish). Then you can make up your own play or stories using your puppet. This is reusable art — what fun!

Dinosaur Puppet

This fun dinosaur puppet was made from an old sock, paint and various household items.

1 Find an old sock, some bright yarn, spare buttons, scraps of fabric (or felt), felt tip pens or paint, and some cotton balls (be sure to ask permission if these items don't belong to you).

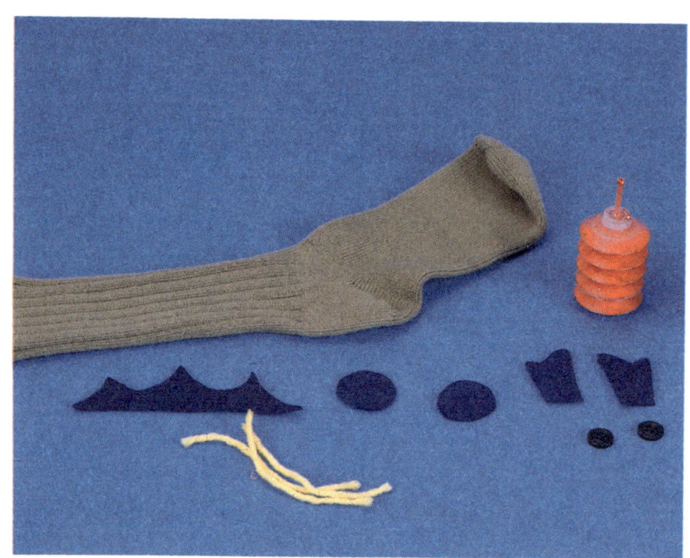

2 Put cotton balls in the toe of the sock to make the head and then put the sock over your hand as if it was already a puppet. Use a pen to mark the positions for the eyes, the mouth, and the back fin.

3 Cut the eyes, the back fin and the front legs out of felt or another fabric. You can copy our example or create your own.

4 Glue the felt and button eyes on the marked spots. (We used squeeze paint instead of glue.) Hold the eyes in place until they stick.

5 Glue on the back fin and front legs. Hold them in place until they stick.

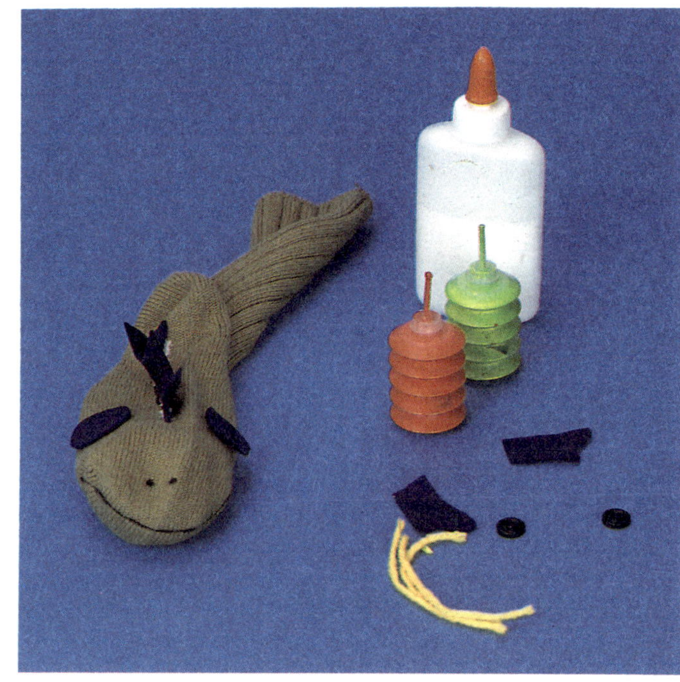

6 Glue on yarn whiskers. Hold them in place until they stick.

7 Let the glue dry completely.

8 If you like, you can use felt tip pens or puff paint to add detail to the eyes, nose, mouth and fin, as shown.

Now you're ready for a fun puppet show!

Woolly Lamb

This cute woolly lamb was made with cotton balls, an empty paper towel tube and felt.

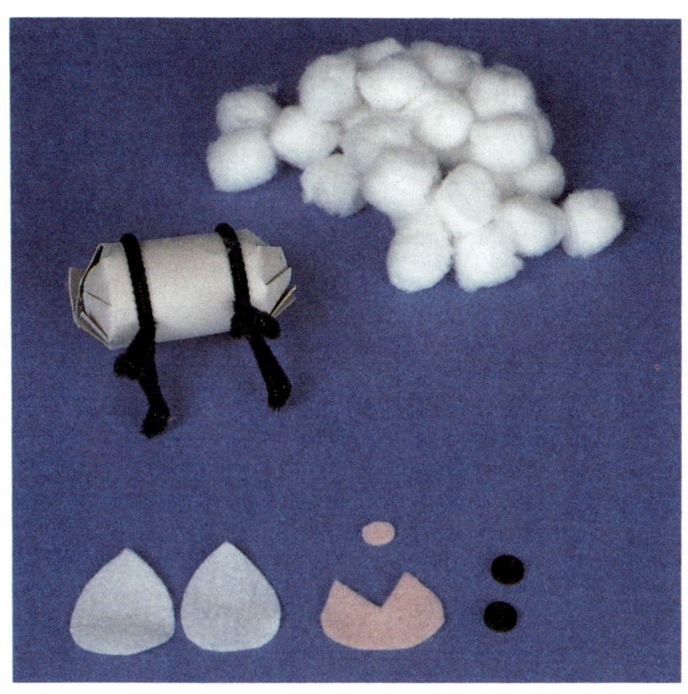

1 Cut an empty paper towel tube in half, or cut one inch off of an empty bathroom tissue roll.

2 Cut slits in the ends of the tube (this makes it easier to bend) and fold in the ends, as shown.

3 Use black pipe cleaners to make legs for the lamb. Wrap them around the tube and twist them together, as shown.

4 Use white glue to attach as many cotton balls as possible to the roll. This will be the lamb's body.

5 Cut two ears, the face and a nose out of felt.

6 Pinch the ears together at one end and glue them together (this makes them look more like ears).

7 Glue the ears to the body. Hold them in place until they stick.

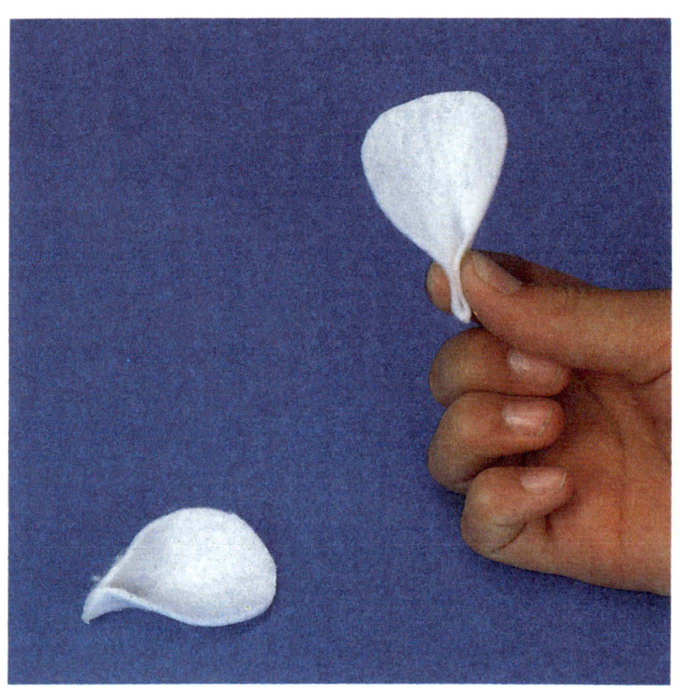

8 Glue on the felt face and the nose. Hold them in place until they stick.

9 Let the glue dry completely.

10 Glue on black button eyes. Hold them in place until they stick.

11 Let the glue dry completely.

Baa! Baa! Baa!

Beach Bag

We made this colorful beach bag with a large piece of raw canvas and acrylic paint.

1 Cut out a piece of canvas twice as large as you want the finished bag to be. (Fold the canvas in half to see how it will look.) The example shown is 34" x 30" flat, or 17" x 30" folded.

2 Cut strips in both sides — 2" wide and 5" long, as shown. We cut eight on each side.

3 Cut out four separate handles — 4" wide and 30" long.

TOP

FOLD

CUT CUT

CUT CUT

CUT CUT

CUT CUT

CUT CUT

CUT CUT

CUT CUT

CENTER FOLD

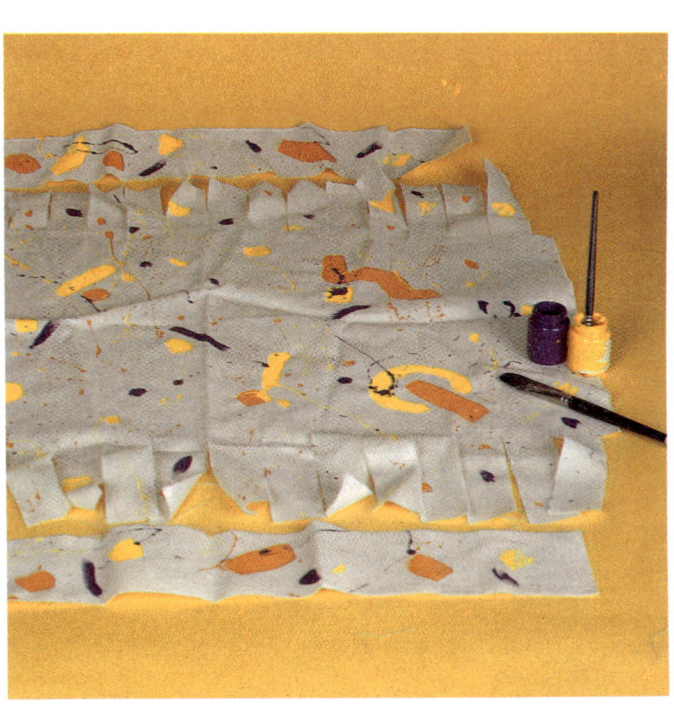

4 Lay the fabric out on a clean, flat surface. Note — the paint will bleed through the fabric, so make sure you put paper (such as newspaper) underneath it. With the pieces laying flat, use acrylic paint to decorate each piece. Use your imagination! We brushed and splattered watered-down paint on ours. This can be very messy, so be careful! (Ask permission first.) You may want to do it outdoors.

5 Let the paint dry completely.

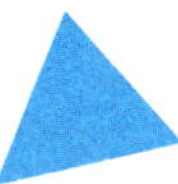

6 Fold the top edge over and use iron-on tape or sew it for a finished edge.

7 Fold the canvas in half to form the bag. Tie the strips on the sides together, as shown.

8 Fold each of the 30" handles lengthwise, then fold the edges in so they meet in the middle. Use an iron to make them stay. (You might want to ask an adult for help.) Tie a knot in the middle of each one, as we did.

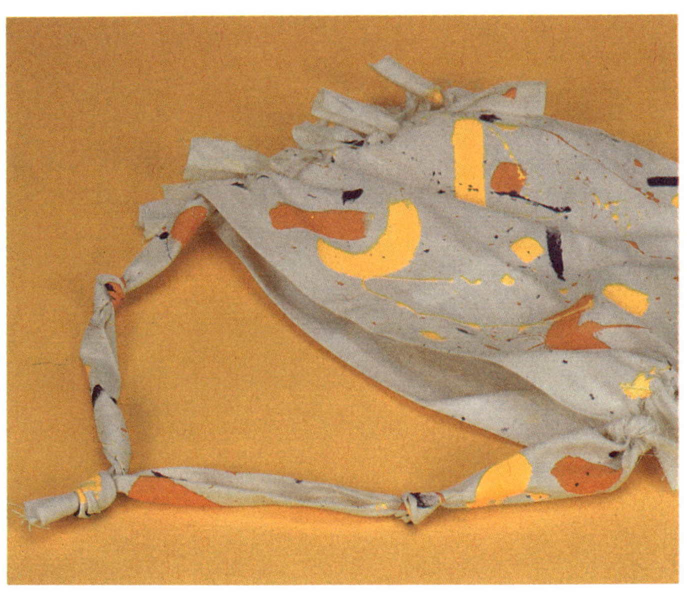

9 Tie two handles together to make one long handle, then tie the other two together to make a second handle.

10 Tie these two long handles to the beach bag.

Let's go to the beach!

Masquerade Mask

We used canvas, pipe cleaners, acrylic paint, glitter glue, and rhinestones to make this fun mask.

1 Use acrylics to paint a piece of canvas white on both sides.

2 Let the paint dry completely.

3 Use pencil to draw the mask shape on the painted canvas.

4 Carefully cut out the mask and the eye holes.

5 Lightly draw a design on the mask with pencil. Use your imagination!

6 Choose bright, fun colors to paint your design. Use as many sizes, shapes and colors as you wish!

7 Let the paint dry completely.

8 Glue pipe cleaners around the edge of the mask. Hold them in place until they stick.

9 Let the glue dry completely.

10 Curl some pipe cleaners by wrapping them around your finger or a pencil, then glue them to the top of the mask. Hold them in place until they stick.

11 Let the glue dry completely.

12 Now decorate the mask with glitter glue, as shown.

13 You may want to add rhinestones and imitation pearls — just stick them into the wet glitter glue.

14 Staple a stick to one side, as we did, or attach a string to each side to tie it around your head.

Guess who?!

United Kingdom Flag

This flag was made out of nylon fabric and acrylic paint.
You can make any kind of flag you wish!

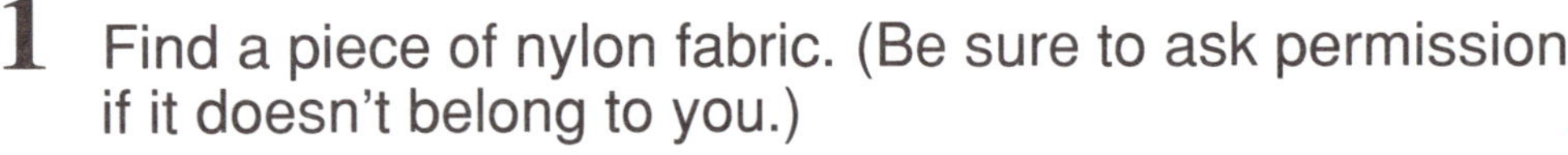

1 Find a piece of nylon fabric. (Be sure to ask permission if it doesn't belong to you.)

2 Cut out the flag, allowing an extra inch on all four sides. For example, if you want the finished flag to be 18" x 24", cut out a piece 20" x 26".

3 Use pencil to draw the design on the flag. You may want to copy a design from a book or create your own.

4 Tape the flag to a piece of cardboard or poster board.

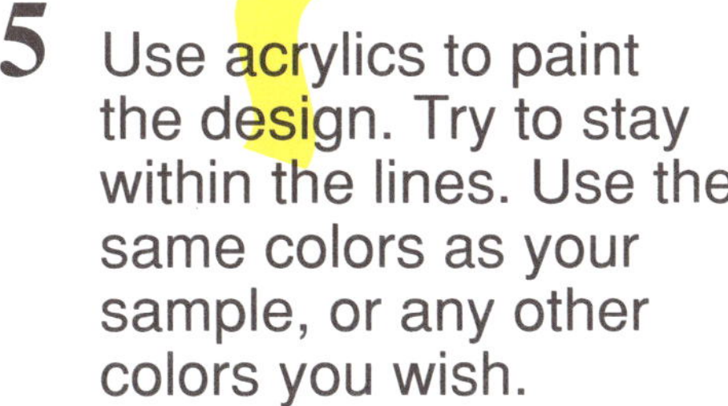

5 Use acrylics to paint the design. Try to stay within the lines. Use the same colors as your sample, or any other colors you wish.

6 Let the paint dry completely.

7 Trim the flag so it is even on all sides.

8 Glue a stick handle to the flag, as shown.

Decorative Pillow

This fancy pillow can be made with raw canvas (or heavy cotton) and paint.

1 Cut two identical squares out of your fabric or canvas. Leave an extra half-inch on each side for the seam. For example, our finished pillow is 24" x 24" so we cut out a 25" x 25" piece of fabric.

2 Use acrylics to paint designs on both pieces of fabric. You may want to choose colors that will match your room. We used a brush to splatter watered-down paint on our example. This can be very messy, so be careful! You may want to lay down newspaper or do it outdoors.

3 Let the paint dry completely.

4 Place the painted sides of the fabric together and use a needle and thread to sew three sides together. Be careful! You might want to ask an adult for help.

5 Turn the pillow right-side-out and fill it with fiberfill, old, clean rags, or cotton.

6 Carefully sew the fourth side shut.

Be prepared! Decorators will be calling you for your designer pillows!

Tic-Tac-Toe Game

This fun game was made with brightly-colored felt. Traditionally, Tic-Tac-Toe uses Xs and Os, but there is no reason why you can't make stars or any other shapes you want! Use your imagination!

1 Cut out a large square of felt and an identical piece of cardboard or poster board.

2 Glue the felt to the cardboard or poster board.

3 Let the glue dry completely.

4 Cut four strips for the crisscross lines out of different colors of felt.

5 Glue the crisscross lines on the square background, as shown.

6 Let the glue dry completely.

7 Draw five identical designs on a different color of felt, then cut them out. These will be one person's game pieces.

8 Draw five different identical designs on a different color of felt, then cut them out. These will be the other person's game pieces. (You can make different game pieces for each of your friends!)

Who wants to play first?

Fun Door Sign

We made this personalized door sign out of various colors of felt and squeeze paint.

1 Cut out a square piece of felt and an identical piece of cardboard or poster board. We made our example 8" x 10".

2 Glue the felt to the cardboard or poster board. Let the glue dry completely.

3 Use pencil to draw the letters of your name on different pieces of felt. Use bright, fun colors! We used a different color and style for each letter.

4 Cut out the letters.

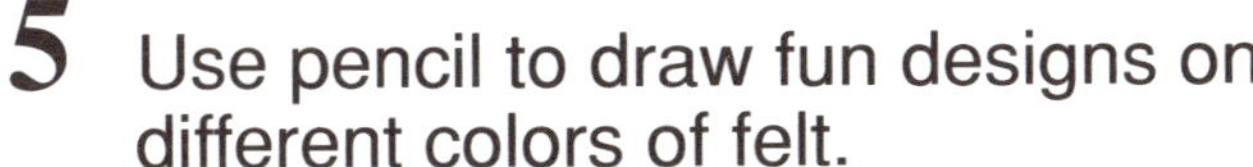

5 Use pencil to draw fun designs on different colors of felt.

6 Cut out the designs.

7 Arrange the letters and the designs on the square felt. When you are pleased with the arrangement, glue them down.

8 If you wish, you can add more designs with squeeze or glitter paint.

9 Let the glue and the paint dry completely.

10 Ask permission to tape or hang the sign on your bedroom door. We used yarn to hang our sign.

Now all your friends can find your room!

JESS

2 GIFTS

There is something extra special about a handmade gift. We especially feel this way about fabric art because it has the added characteristic of being soft. And, you will find that even though these gifts are inexpensive, they will be treasured for many years. (That's another nice feature of fabric art — with care, it usually lasts a long time.)

Remember, you don't need a holiday or a special occasion to give a somebody present — a gift just to show someone you appreciate them is sometimes the nicest gift of all.

Our projects are just ideas we came up with, but you can use your imagination to make anything you wish. Use our directions or change them to make your own design. Art is even more fun when it is a gift for someone you like. **Have fun!**

Kitchen Towels

We used plain white kitchen towels (or plain white fabric) and acrylic paints to make these fancy fruit-print kitchen towels. They make a great gift!

1 Practice making different designs on a piece of scratch paper. Decide which design you like best, then proceed to step two.

2 Lay the towel or fabric out on a clean, dry surface. (be sure to ask permission if the towels do not belong to you!) The paint will bleed through the fabric so be sure to lay paper (such as waxed paper) underneath it.

3 Cut two lemons in half, then cut one of the halves in half again. (You can also use oranges, limes or any kind of citrus fruit — use your imagination!)

4 Put acrylic paints into different saucer-like dishes or lids. Note — the paint may not wash out very well, so be sure to get permission first. (Glass containers are the best.)

5 One at a time, dip the lemon sections into the paint. Remove any excess by pressing them onto a piece of scratch paper or newspaper. Then press the lemon onto the towel, as shown. Use a different lemon section for each color.

6 Patiently and carefully repeat the process until you are satisfied with the design. You may want to try overlapping the patterns.

7 You can use a paint brush to add to the design or to write the name of the person that you are giving them to.

Decorative Box

This pretty box was made out of a cardboard box, fabric, paint, rhinestones and ribbon.

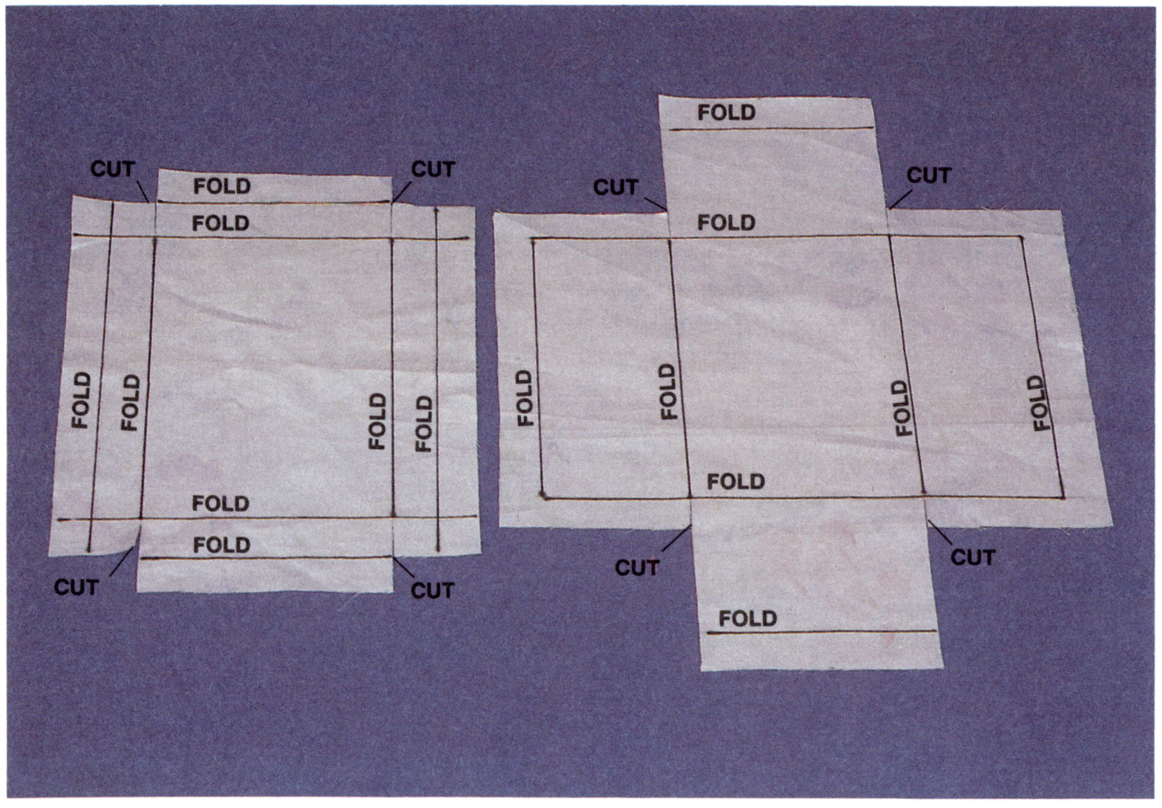

1 Cut out a piece of fabric large enough to cover your cardboard box. (Wrap the cloth around the box before you cut it to make sure it covers the box completely.)

2 Cut out a piece of fabric to cover the lid.

3 Cut out the corners, as shown.

4 Use a medium size artist's paint brush to spread white glue all over the outside of the box. Carefully wrap the fabric around the box and pull it tight. Smooth it out with your fingers.

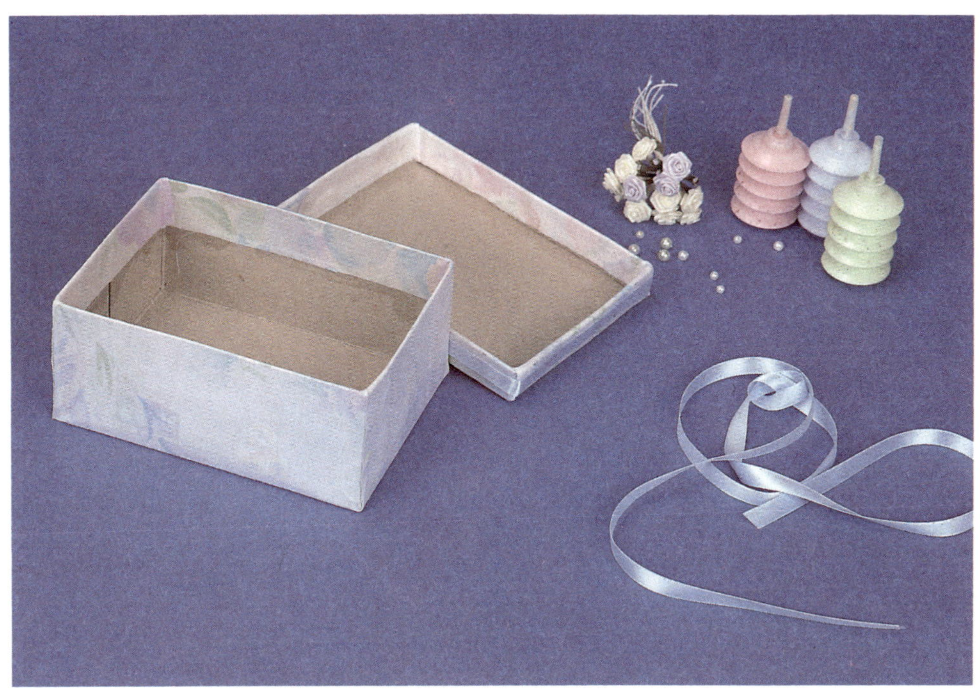

5 Use the same method to cover the lid with fabric.

6 Glue ribbons, rhinestones or whatever you want to the box and the lid. Use your imagination!

7 You may want to decorate the lid with puff paint — or write somebody's name on the lid!

8 Add imitation pearls or rhinestones by pushing them into the wet puff paint.

What a great birthday gift for your sister or a friend!

Door Snake

This funny door snake was made of raw canvas (or heavy fabric) and acrylic paint.

Door snakes are used in the winter to prevent cold air from blowing under the door; they may even stifle noise from a stereo. But they are also fun to play with!

1 Fold a piece of fabric in half lengthwise.

2 Use pencil to draw the outline of the snake. (By folding the fabric in half, both halves of the snake will be identical.)

3 Cut out the snake design, as shown. Now you will have two identical pieces.

4 Turn the fabric inside-out and use simple, straight stitches to sew the sides of the snake together. (Be careful! You might want to ask an adult for help.) This will make the snake round, like a tube.

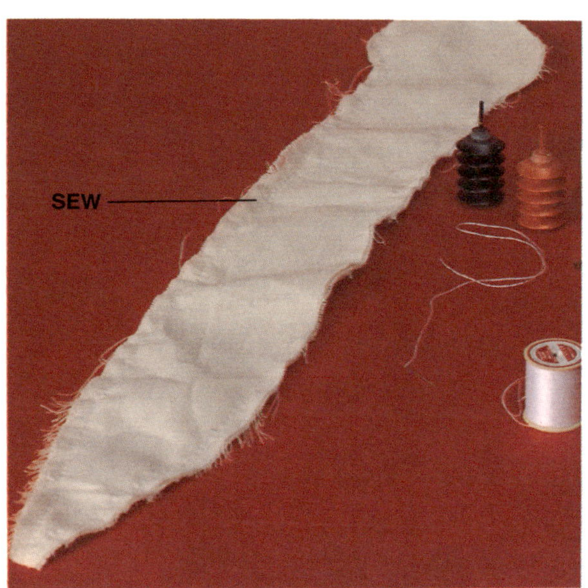

5 Turn the snake right-side-out.

6 Stuff the snake with fiberfill, rags, or cotton.

7 Carefully sew the ends shut.

8 Use a sponge to paint colorful designs on the fabric, as shown.

9 You can use squeeze paint, a paint brush or anything you wish to decorate your snake. Be creative!

10 Let the paint dry.

What a great gift!

Fabric Picture Frame

This pretty frame was made with cardboard, acrylic paint, fabric, glue, ribbon and silk flowers.

1 Carefully cut a frame out of cardboard. Ours is 7 1/2" x 9 1/2" with a 5" x 7" opening.

2 Lay the fabric out flat with the decorative side down.

3 Lay your cardboard frame on top of the cloth.

4 Lightly trace around the frame with pencil. Trace the outside and the inside of the frame.

5 Leaving an extra inch around the pencil lines, as shown, cut out the fabric.

6 Cut notches in the corners of the fabric. This will make it easier to wrap the fabric.

7 Glue cottons balls evenly onto the cardboard frame. This will make the frame puffy.

8 Lay the frame cotton ball side down on the fabric.

9 Apply glue to the back of the cardboard frame. Use a paint brush to spread it evenly.

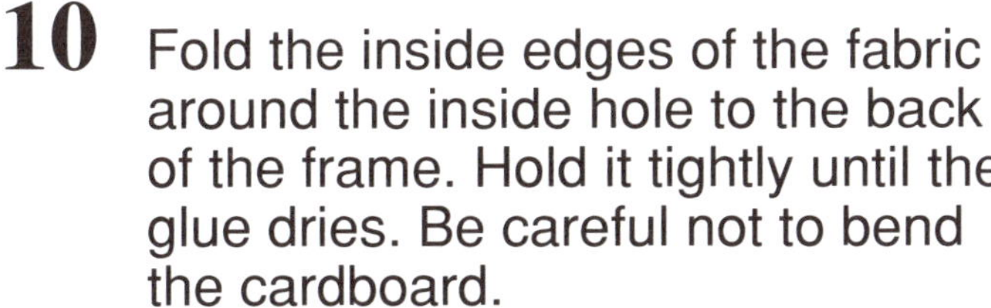

10 Fold the inside edges of the fabric around the inside hole to the back of the frame. Hold it tightly until the glue dries. Be careful not to bend the cardboard.

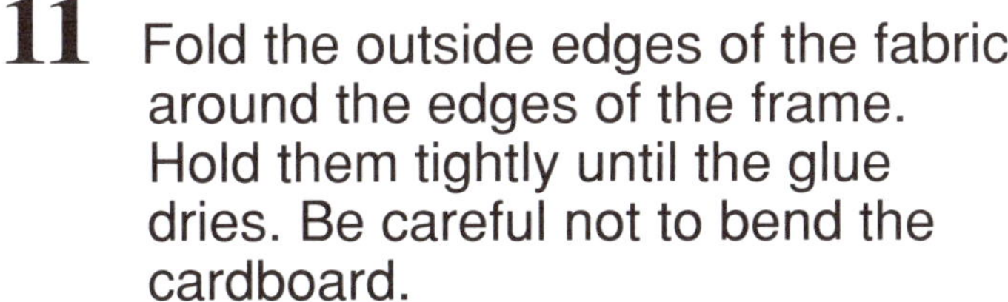

11 Fold the outside edges of the fabric around the edges of the frame. Hold them tightly until the glue dries. Be careful not to bend the cardboard.

12 Now decorate the frame. Use your imagination!

13 We glued lace to the outside edges.

14 We also glued silk flowers onto the upper left corner. If the flowers don't match the frame, you can paint over them with acrylic paint. (This makes the flowers look like porcelain.)

15 We tied a ribbon into a bow, then painted it with acrylic paint and glued it on.

Now add a fun photo of your family or friends!

MOM
ARIN

3

HOLIDAY FUN

The best holiday decorations are ones that have been handmade. People appreciate all the work and creativity that goes into making them. And, when the holiday is over you can pack them away until the next year. Over the years these fabric art projects will bring back a lot of memories and happiness when you pull them out and think about how you made them years before. (That is a nice feature of fabric art — most of these projects will last for years.)

Of course, you can also use these directions to make decorations for any occasion or just to decorate your room (the wind sock is a good example). Just change the colors and the designs.

Remember, you are limited only by your imagination! **Have fun!**

Fourth of July Wind Sock

This festive wind sock was made with nylon fabric, paint and flexible wire. You can make a wind sock for any holiday or occasion!

1 Cut out a piece of lightweight nylon fabric. Ours is 21" wide and 44" long.

2 Use a pencil to draw 17" slits about three inches apart on one end of the fabric, as shown.

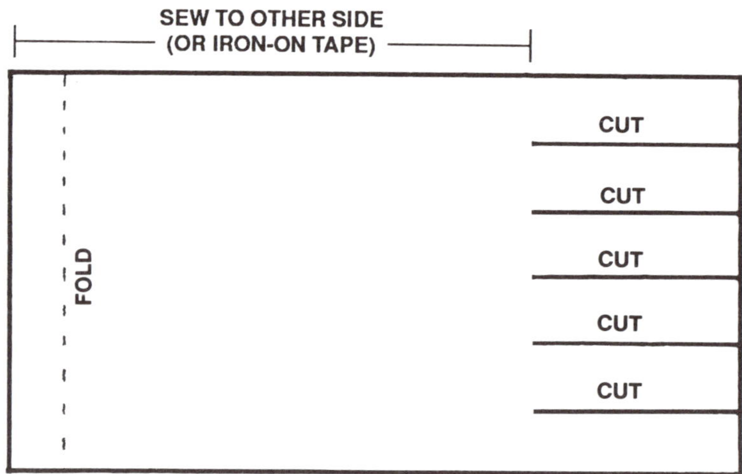

3 Use a stencil to decorate the fabric. (You can buy stencils or make your own by cutting patterns out of card-board)

4 Paint stars by dipping a sponge into a dish of paint and then over the stencil onto the fabric, as shown. (Use a clean sponge for each color.)

5 We made red stripes on our flag by dipping a sponge into acrylic paint and carefully painting along the 17" pencil lines (this will prevent the fabric from unraveling).

6 Let the paint dry thoroughly.

7 Cut along the pencil lines through the red stripes.

8 Now fold the top end of the fabric down 1" and sew it (you can also use iron-on tape). Be sure to leave a small opening so you can insert the wire.

9 Fold the fabric lengthwise with the painted side on the inside and either sew the edges together or use iron-on tape (we used iron-on tape for our example).

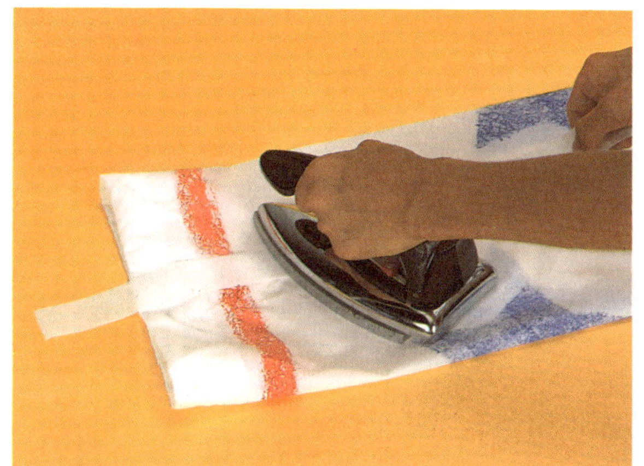

10 Turn the sock right-side-out.

11 Run flexible wire through the top of the tube, as shown. Bend it to make it round.

12 Attach a piece of string (about 15") to the top of the sock to make a handle, as shown.

13 Attach another piece of string to the middle of the other string, as shown. Now hang it outside so it can catch the wind!

Rag Christmas Wreath

We chose to make our wreath with green polka dotted fabric, a red ribbon bow, puff paint and jingle bells. But remember, you can decorate yours with anything you wish! Use your imagination!

1 Cut three 1" strips out of your fabric. We cut ours at an angle, as shown, so they will wrap better.

2 Wrap each fabric strip around a 36" piece of thick rope or wire. (You may need to ask a friend to hold one end for you.)

3 Tape both ends, as shown.

4 Braid the three 36" pieces, then tape the two ends together.

5 Make a red ribbon bow for the top.

6 We chose to tie smaller red ribbon bows at the sides and the bottom.

7 Glue the red bow to the top of the wreath (where the ends meet).

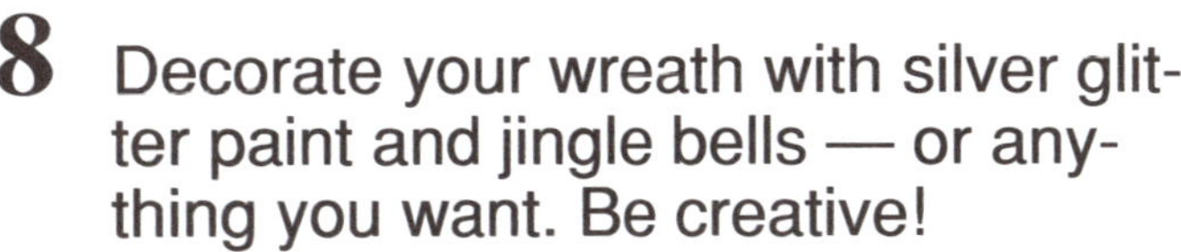

8 Decorate your wreath with silver glitter paint and jingle bells — or anything you want. Be creative!

What a wonderful Christmas decoration!

Valentine Candy Jar

This fancy candy jar was made out of an empty jar with a lid, fabric, lace, cotton, ribbon, fabric paint, and puff paint.

1 Using the lid of the jar as a pattern, trace a circle on a piece of pink or red fabric.

2 Leaving an extra 1/2" all the way around, cut out the fabric. For example, our lid is 3 1/2", so we cut out a 4 1/2" piece of fabric. (This extra fabric will be glued to the sides of the lid.)

3 Glue cotton balls to the top of the lid, as shown. This will make the lid puffy. Let the glue dry thoroughly.

4 Put glue around the edge of the lid and place the round piece of fabric over the cotton balls. Press the fabric to the sides of the lid.

5 Use a rubber band to hold the fabric in place.

6 Let the glue dry thoroughly.

7 Glue the lace ruffle over the rubber band.

8 Glue or tie a ribbon around the edge of the lace and around the lid. (You may also want to tie a bow as we have.)

9 We cut a heart shape out of matching fabric and glued it to the lid.

10 Using white and red puff paint, add designs to the lid and the jar.

11 Let the paint dry completely.

12 Now you can fill the jar with your favorite candy, game pieces, trinkets, etc.

This makes a great gift for Valentine's Day!

Spider and Web

All you need for this scary Halloween decoration is string, glue and black acrylic paint!

WEB

1 Draw a spider web on a large piece of paper. Ours is 24" x 24".

2 Cut several pieces of heavy string that fit the web drawing. Paint the string with black acrylic paint.

3 Let the paint dry thoroughly.

4 Lay each piece of string over the drawing of the web.

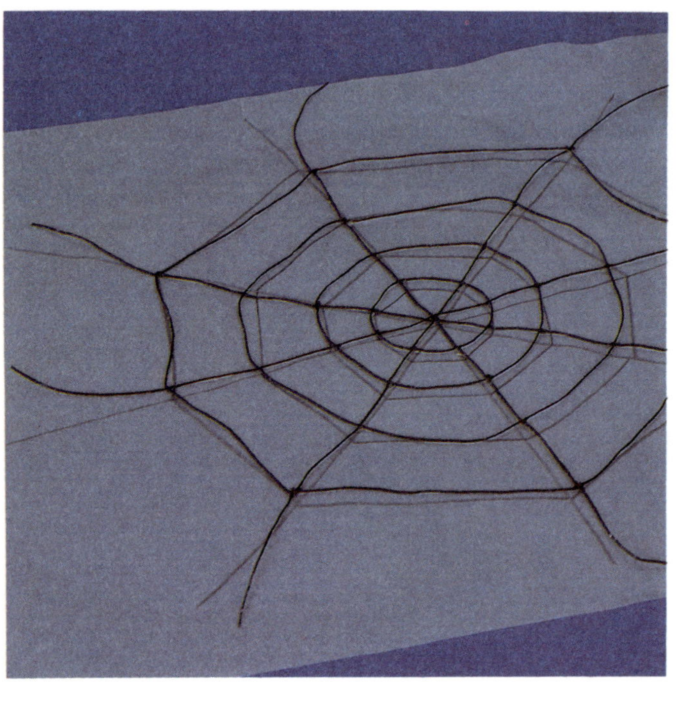

5 Put a single drop of glue on each spot where the strings overlap, as shown.

6 Let the glue dry thoroughly.

7 Carefully turn the spider web over and glue the other side.

8 Let the glue dry completely.

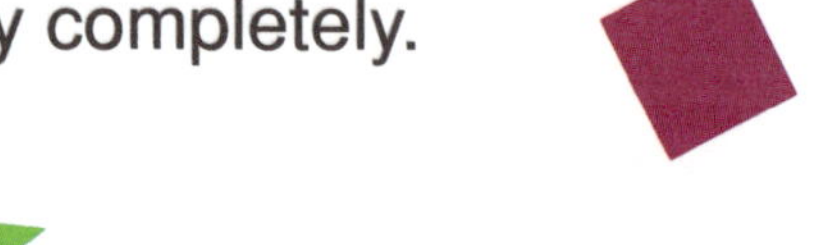

SPIDER

1. Measure and cut four 4" pieces of string.
2. Tie the four pieces of string together with a double knot in the center. (The knot is the spider's body.)
3. Trim the legs so they are all the same length (about 1 1/4").
4. Glue the double knot together. Let the glue dry thoroughly.
5. Paint the spider with black acrylic paint. Let the paint dry completely.
6. Now glue the spider to the web and hang it up.

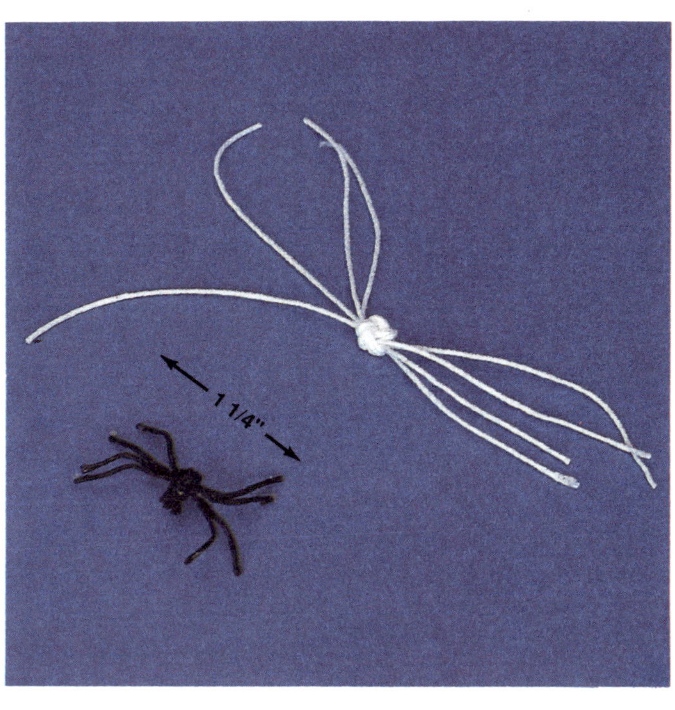

Christmas Stocking

This festive stocking was made with red and green felt, yarn, string or ribbon, fabric or puff paint, and cotton balls.

1. Fold a large piece of red felt in half. Our piece is 18” x 10” folded.
2. Draw a stocking shape on the felt with a felt tip pen.
3. Leaving the fabric folded, cut out the stocking shape. This will give you two identical pieces for your stocking.
4. Use a hole punch to punch holes all the way around the stocking, except at the top. We punched one piece of felt first, then marked the other one through the holes and punched it in the same places.

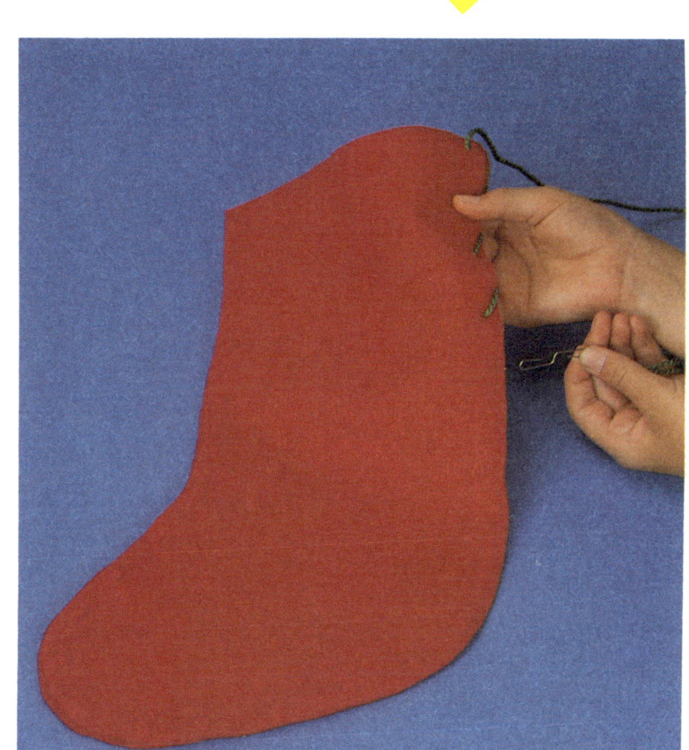

5 Thread ribbon or yarn through the holes to hold the pieces of the stocking together, as shown. We used a paper clip as a "needle." Be sure to leave extra yarn at the top to make the handle.

6 Draw holly shapes on green felt, then cut them out.

7 Glue the green holly onto the red stocking.

8 Use puff paint to write your name at the top. Or, you might want to make one for someone else.

9 If you wish, add glitter and red rhinestones to the stocking. We added a red rhinestone to make a holly berry.

10 Glue cotton balls to the top of the stocking.

11 Let the glue dry thoroughly.

Santa Claus won't miss these wonderfully soft stockings!

Felt Greeting Card

These fun cards were made with cookie cutters, different colors of felt, squeeze paint, acrylic paint or puff paint, and yarn.

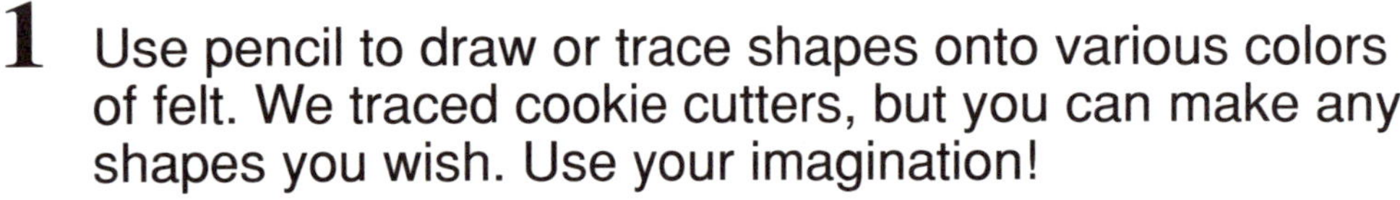

1. Use pencil to draw or trace shapes onto various colors of felt. We traced cookie cutters, but you can make any shapes you wish. Use your imagination!
2. Carefully cut out the shapes.
3. Fold a piece of drawing or construction paper in half. This will be the card. Use any color you wish!
4. Glue the felt shapes on the front of the card.
5. Let the glue dry thoroughly.

6 Use pencil to carefully write your message on the front of the card.

7 Trace over the pencil lines with puff paint. If you choose, you can write your message on the inside and just make decorations on the outside.

8 Decorate the felt shapes with puff paint or squeeze paint.

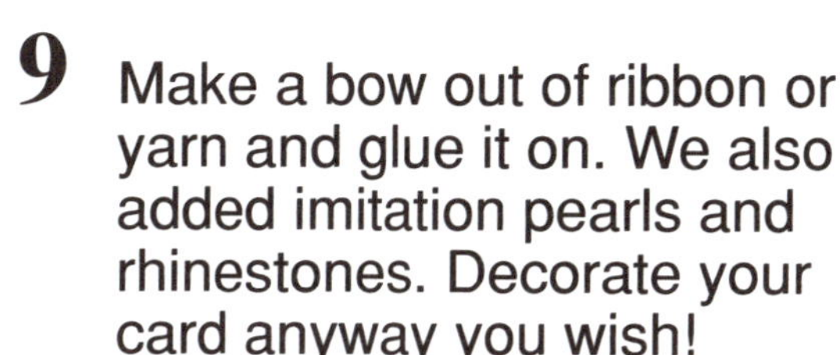

9 Make a bow out of ribbon or yarn and glue it on. We also added imitation pearls and rhinestones. Decorate your card anyway you wish!

You can make a greeting card for any holiday or occasion!

4

ART YOU CAN WEAR

This chapter is especially fun because we're going to make art work that you can wear — everywhere you go people will see your art work!

Everyone likes to be unique, and what better way than with your very own, one-of-a-kind, wearable art! No one at school will have a pair of shoes or a sweatshirt exactly like yours. You can use any color schemes or designs you wish. You can even glue on your own decorations — be creative!

There is one important thing to remember when doing the projects in this chapter — plan out your design before you begin! This will prevent disappointment. With a little planning, you can use our directions to create any fashion you want. Just use your imagination and, of course, **have fun!**

Designer Socks

These fancy socks were made with squeeze paint, rhinestones, imitation pearls, buttons, ribbon, lace, etc. (Be sure to ask permission if the materials do not belong to you.)

1. Practice drawing or painting simple designs on a piece of scratch paper. Which design do you like best? We made two different examples.

2. Use puff paint or acrylic paint to paint the design on the cuffs of a pair of socks.

3. Let the paint dry thoroughly.

4. Tie two bows out of ribbon or lace and glue or sew them onto the socks. You may also want to glue on some lace by outlining it with puff paint.

5 While the paint is still wet, push imitation pearls, rhinestones, buttons, etc. into the paint (the paint will act like glue).

6 Hand wash the socks in cold water and hang dry (this will make them last longer). Pearls and rhinestones will stay on in the dryer.

You might become the trendsetter of your school!

Jewelry Pin

This pretty pin was made with fabric, ribbon (or ribbon flowers), glue, cardboard, imitation pearls, puff paint and a jewelry pin. (You can buy the pin at an arts & crafts or hobby store.)

1. Draw a shape on a piece of cardboard or poster board. We made a heart, but you can make any shape you wish.
2. Cut out the cardboard shape.
3. Trace around the cardboard onto a piece of fabric with pencil.
4. Carefully cut out the fabric shape.
5. Glue the fabric to the cardboard. Press any bumps or wrinkles out with your fingers.
6. Let the glue dry completely.
7. You may want to trim the shape so the cardboard and fabric match exactly.

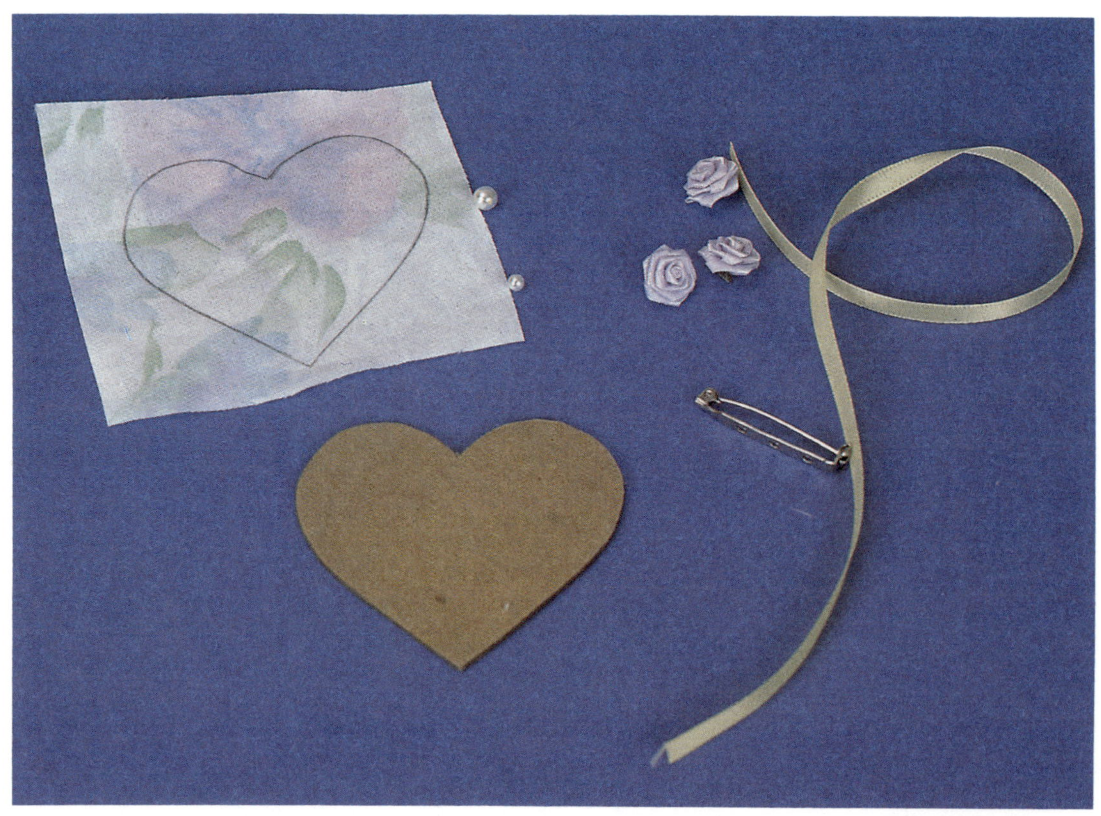

8 Make a bow out of a piece of ribbon and glue it on.

9 Decorate the pin with squeeze or puff paint.

10 Glue the ribbon flowers on by pushing them into the wet puff paint. (You can do the same thing with imitation pearls or rhinestones.)

11 Let the glue and the paint dry thoroughly. (While it is drying, why not make more jewelry?)

12 Glue a jewelry pin to the back, as shown.

13 Let the glue dry thoroughly before pinning it on!

This pin will go well with those socks! What a fashion whiz you are!

Sweatshirt

You will need a sweatshirt, crayons and puff paint to make this unique shirt. (Be sure to wash and dry the sweatshirt first!)

1 Use a pencil to lightly draw designs (shapes) on the sweatshirt. Decide what colors you want to use.

2 Lay the sweatshirt out on a clean, flat surface.

3 Place some paper (such as paper towels) inside the shirt, between the front and the back. (This will prevent the crayons from bleeding through to the back.)

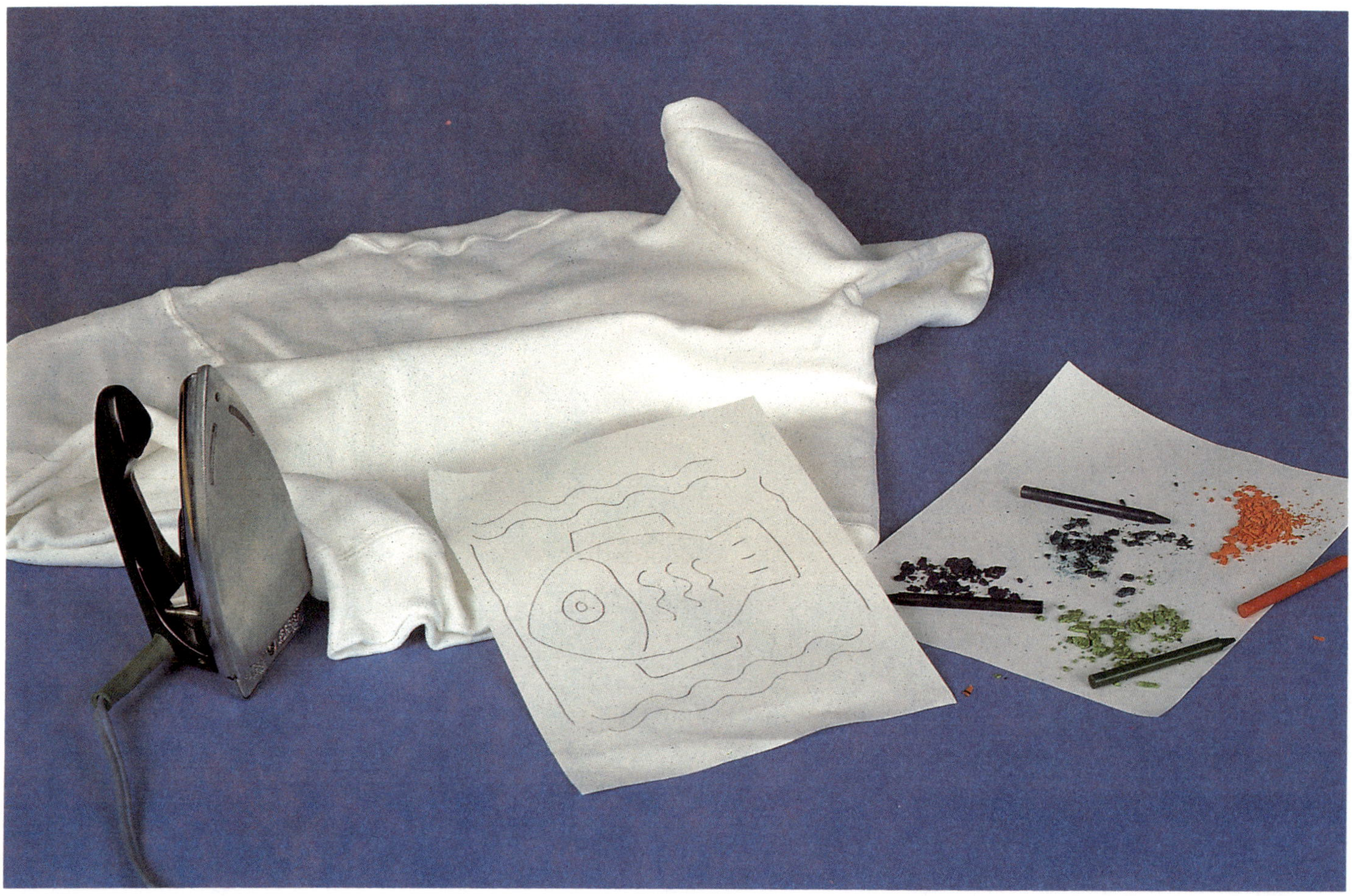

4 Place a crayon between two pieces of waxed paper and crush it. (We rolled over ours with a rolling pin.)

5 Place the crushed pieces of crayon on the area of the shirt where you want that particular color.

6 Place a couple of paper towels over the smashed crayon and iron it until the crayon melts. You may want to ask an adult for help.

7 Repeat these steps with the rest of the colors.

8 Outline each design with puff paint.

9 You may want to add more designs with the puff paint.

10 Let the paint dry.

11 Note — In the future, wash the sweatshirt in cold water and hang to dry. Do not use the dryer!

This is definitely one-of-a-kind!

T-Shirt

You will need a t-shirt, iron-on patches, puff paint or squeeze paint, and buttons to make this fun project! (Be sure to wash the t-shirt first!)

1 Use a pencil to draw shapes on the iron-on patches. Use your imagination!

2 Carefully cut out the shapes.

3 Iron the shapes onto your t-shirt (follow the directions for the iron-on patches). You may want to ask an adult for help.

4 Carefully outline each shape with puff paint. Use bright, fun colors!

5 You may want to use puff paint to add more designs to the shirt, as we have.

6 While the paint is still wet, push buttons (or other decorative objects) into the paint wherever you think they might look good. When the paint dries it will glue the buttons onto the shirt.

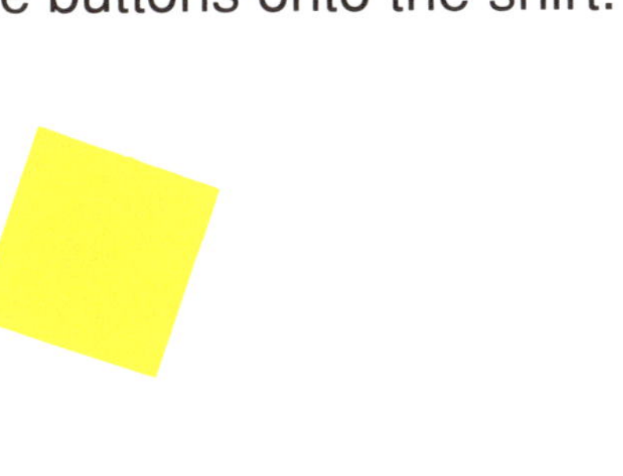

7 Note — In the future, wash the t-shirt in cold water and hang to dry. Do not use the dryer!

What a great summer fashion!

Tennis Shoes

You can make new or old tennis shoes look great! You will need acrylics, puff paint or squeeze paint, rhinestones, imitation pearls, and buttons. (Be sure to ask permission if the materials do not belong to you.)

1 If you are using an old pair of shoes, clean them well and let dry.

2 Practice drawing or painting designs on a piece of scratch paper. Use different shapes and colors. Decide which design you like best. (We made two different examples.)

3 Using light pencil, carefully draw your favorite design on each shoe.

4 Now use acrylic, squeeze or puff paint to paint over the designs.

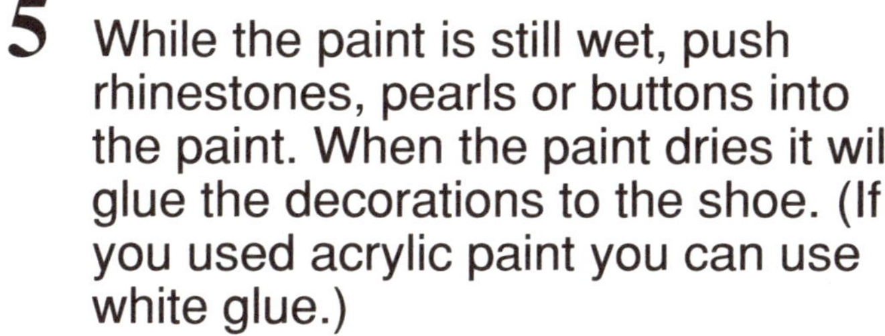

5 While the paint is still wet, push rhinestones, pearls or buttons into the paint. When the paint dries it will glue the decorations to the shoe. (If you used acrylic paint you can use white glue.)

6 Let the paint dry thoroughly.

7 Repeat the above steps until the shoes look the way you want them to.

Now you can wear your fancy new shoes!

Multi-Colored Shoelaces

We used acrylic paints to make these multi-colored shoelaces. Choose colors to complement your favorite outfits!

1 Lay a pair of shoelaces out on a clean piece of paper.

2 Thin various colors of acrylic paint with water and put them into different bowls. (You can also use fabric paint.) Ask permission if the bowls do not belong to you.

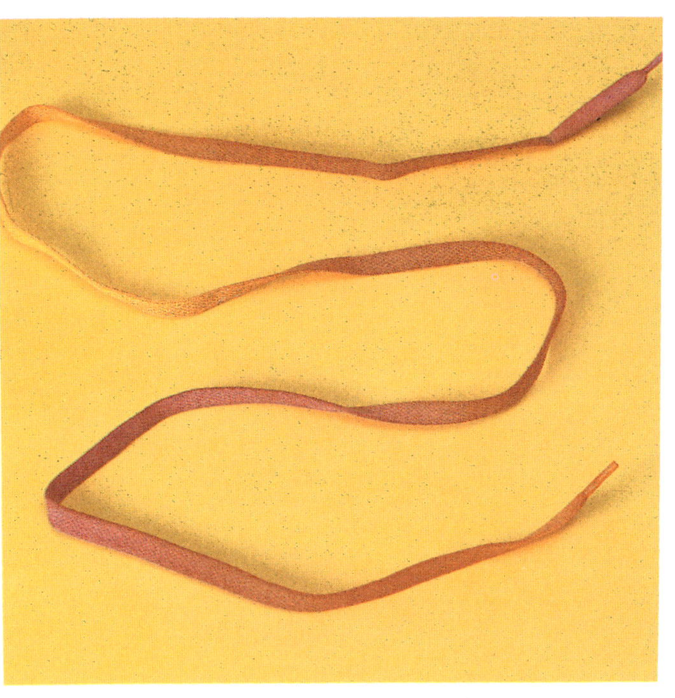

3 Dip different sections of the shoelaces into the bowls of paint. (This is similar to dyeing Easter eggs.)

4 Lay the laces out on the paper and let them dry.

What fun!

Pastel Shoelaces

Here's another fun way to decorate shoelaces — with squeeze and puff paints! Try both methods and see which one you like best!

1 Lay a pair of shoelaces out on a clean piece of paper.

2 Use squeeze paint to make designs on the shoelaces. Be creative!

3 Let the paint dry completely.

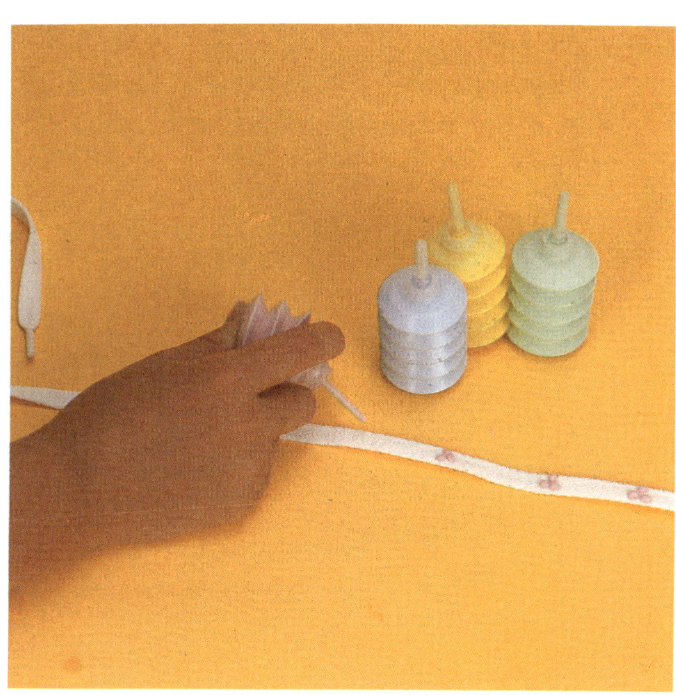

4 Use puff paint to dot colors on your laces. Let the paint dry.

5 You may want to get really wild and first paint your laces as we did on the previous page and then decorate them as we have on this page.

Who says shoelaces are boring!?

Beginners Art Series

Walter Foster's **Beginners Art Series** is a great way to introduce children to the wonderful world of art. Designed for ages 6 and up, this popular new series helps children develop strong tactile and visual skills while having lots of fun! Each book explores a different medium and features exciting "hands-on" projects with simple step-by-step instructions.

- **Drawing Fun** begins with basic shapes children know, and progresses to instruction on shading, shadows, and perspective.
- **Color Fun** teaches the fundamentals of color theory: color identification, color mixing, and color schemes.
- **Clay Fun** demonstrates clay sculpting techniques, and acquaints children with several different types of clay.
- **Comic Strip Fun** teaches children how to draw facial expressions, body movements and character interaction.
- **Poster Fun** introduces basic design and lettering skills, then uses these techniques to create posters, greeting cards, and games.
- **Paper Art Fun** shows how to create a variety of paper art objects from everyday materials like construction paper and paper bags.
- **Cartoon Fun** teaches beginning artists how to use simple shapes to create cartoon characters.
- **Painting Fun** teaches the fundamentals of painting with watercolor, acrylic, oil, and poster paints.
- **Felt Tip Fun** demonstrates the use of a variety of felt tip and marker pens through projects ranging from two-dimensional art to a puppet and a diorama.
- **Colored Pencil Fun** offers a series of two- and three-dimensional art projects which help children learn fundamentals such as shading, color blending, and basic drawing.

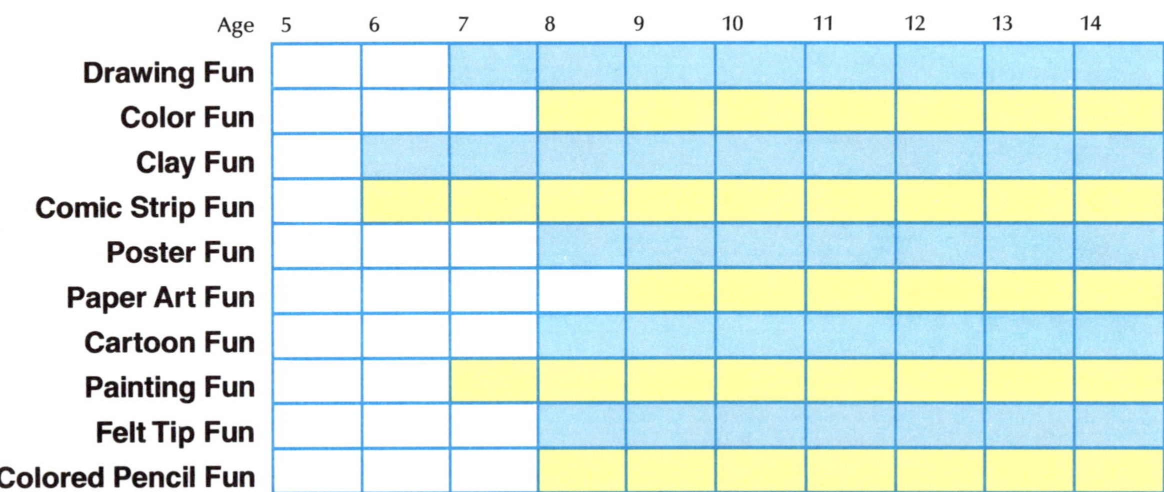